Jesus In Me

Worship Poems For Kids

Ana Blair, M.Ed.

Printed in the United States of America

First Printing, 2017

ISBN ISBN-13: 978-1-948605-01-4

Pataskity Publishing

Augusta, Georgia

Ana Blair

SPEAKER TEACHER AUTHOR

GEORGIA

Table Of Contents

Crystal Christ..1

Lord, Here Am I..2

May I?...3

The Lord Will Always Care...4

A Mansion in Your Kingdom...5

Because I Love You...6

Loving & Living In Christ...7

Joyful Song...8

Strength...9

Think and Consider..10

Dreams of a Kid...11

One Prayer..12

Life...13

A Rose..14

Even If I Must Cry...15

Show Me The Way...16

An Open Door..17

My Ten Facts...18

If...19

Crystal Christ

You are like crystal inside of me

Because you make me pure.

Sometimes among my friends, I don't want you to shine,

But you are so pure I choose not to mind

Because you are all knowing,

And through your eyes, my heart is seen.

Crystal Christ,

Sometimes I don't want to give,

But in you, I cannot selfishly live.

Sometimes I don't want to smile,

But because of your love, I laugh out loud.

You have taught me to embrace life,

And let go of the brokenness of my past.

Crystal Christ,

You are the Crystal of my eyes

And the joy of my life.

Lord, Here Am I

Lord, here I stand.

If you need me, call my name.

Lord, hear me when I pray

That I never go astray.

Lord, when I sing my song

I never want to go wrong because in you is where I belong.

Lord, help me when I read

To understand and not be deceived.

Lord, I pray always to be humble,

And to seek you if I should stumble.

May I?

Not mines to hold,

But yours to share.

Not mines to mold,

But I want to care.

I know your life is cold

Because your soul is afraid.

My Beloved, may I care,

And give you the better life that I share?

All of your burdens I will bear,

But I cannot be there

Until you answer my cry.

May I?

That is what Jesus Christ asks every day.

His promises will never fade away,

So let us respond when Christ cries

To you and I.

The Lord Will Always Care

I don't know about tomorrow.

It may bring joy or sorrow.

Perhaps my goals don't reach fame,

My love for Christ will still be the same.

God is joy when I am in despair,

And I take comfort knowing that his love is sincere.

All of the burdens he will bear.

Whenever no one is there,

Christ will always care.

A Mansion in Your Kingdom

If knowledge does not reach me,

If love does not obtain,

If mercy cannot save me,

If peace will cease,

Lord, please let me enter heaven.

When the sun has faded away,

And nature reproaches herself.

When there is no more, I could do or say

Lord, I hope to make it to heaven all the way.

When my eyes no longer see, nor my tongue speak

Lord, remember my works and that I was meek.

I hope to taste your milk and honey,

And live in your land where there is plenty.

A mansion in your kingdom

Is all I ask through redemption.

Because I Love You

If I were a flower

And you were a butterfly

I will always land on you.

If I were the sun

And you were the moon

I would always prepare day for night.

If I was St.Claire

I would tell St. Micheal

To blow his trumpet for you.

If I owned the planets,

I would give you Jupiter and Uranus.

If I owned the rainbow,

I would let you choose its colors,

However; I am only me

So I will say I love you dearly!

Loving & Living In Christ

God it is you who I love

Who am I kidding?

Without you, my life is not worth living.

You are like flavor to salt.

My life's purpose is to exalt

Your name high because you brought salvation.

Therefore, I should never wonder in hesitation.

Because of your persecution

I can receive redemption.

I can never escape your grace.

I can never get away from your love.

I love living life in a new found way.

Joyful Song

Blue skies and beautiful rainbows

In my soul, a joyful song flows.

When I met you, I asked you to come in my life

You entered within and removed all strife.

Whoever knew that you would be around for so long?

Whenever I go my own way, you keep holding on.

I do not love you for what you give to me,

But I chose you because of who you are to me.

You are rest when I can't sleep,

And joy when I have pain.

You lift me like words that are sweet.

Your grace is like sunshine after rain.

I will love you my whole life through.

I love you; I do!

Strength

Lord, give me the strength to do all that you ask of me.

Open my eyes that I may see.

Teach me about the power of your might.

If you give me your spirit, I can live right.

Your grace

Is all that my heart chase.

Bless me to behold your beauty

And to sail upon your shores of love when life is empty.

Because I am your child, all I ask is that you make me

To live as glorious as you had in mind when you created me.

Think and Consider

If the stars are plentiful

And the nights are impossibly dull,

But you know not Christ

Is it not vanity?

If one obtains silver and gold,

But never committed their soul

What does it profit him?

If one desires the sun and moon,

And obtained them both-,

But missed Christ

What would become of their life?

Stop, Think & Consider

The wondrous works of God

That we may have eternal life.

Dreams of a Kid

As kids, we dream

And pray that the sun will beam.

When we are kids, we never let go

Of promises we believe are so.

We fight to understand

All of life's commands.

Humbly hearted we yield to Christ in each situation

As a result, we are safely guided to our destination.

It is important to know God as we dream

And to keep trying despite how hard it may seem.

We have to pray for grace in each tomorrow

That we will conquer its sorrow.

One Prayer

If I

Ever I

Had one prayer

I would pray

The face of God to never miss.

If I

Ever I

Had one prayer

I would pray the voice of God

To never miss.

If I

Ever I

Had one prayer

I pray to love the Lord

With all of my heart.

Life

Life is sweet

Especially if Christ we meet.

Life is full of ups and downs,

But it's okay because we are working for our crowns.

Life has wonders and deceivers,

but life also has strong believers.

Life continues after death;

This life cannot be bought with wealth.

A Rose

A rose in the winter to bloom in the spring

A flower to hold,

A thought to cherish.

The sun shining brightly

The wind so light

An eagle picks up their wings to fly through life

The sky is my only limit

Not knowing what tomorrow holds.

"*I can do all things through Christ Jesus who strengthens me.*"

Philippians 4:13

Even If I Must Cry

When the sun rises

And mother nature reproaches herself

When the robins sing beautifully

and life has grown fully

The things I once dreamed about

I no longer doubt

Because I realize

No matter how much I am despise

Every day is another chance; a new try

I am willing to go even if I must cry

Show Me The Way

I am what I am

What I do not know today

Tomorrow, I will strive to learn

What I cannot see today

I pray to open my eyes on tomorrow

My conclusion is:

Lord, show me the way

An Open Door

If you listen to wise sages

You will discover life turning its pages

You will see and learn

Seasons changes and you can achieve what you yearn

Set goals attainable

Unto yourself give hope reliable

You can achieve if you believe

You can prosper if you receive

It is your life

Live it not in strife

Life offers so many opportunities in so many ways

Make the most of them and all your days

Be all you can be

And every vision see.

There is an open door

Make the most of it even if you begin at the core---

My Ten Facts

To show what I have
I must gain what I need.

To be what I want to be
I must see who I am.

To walk, I must crawl
To think I must know.

To have, I must reach
To achieve, I must believe.

To receive I must be open
To be up
I must be down.
To be strengthened I must be weakened,
And to be built up
I must be torn down.

If

If I pray when I'm alone

I could please God with a beautiful tone.

I would live right

I know God will be my bright light.

If I could love and respect all men

God will love and honor me then.

If I grow and have not wealth or fame

My love for God will still be the same.

If I set my affection high

My soul will live after my flesh die

If God's ways I admire

God will give me my heart's desire.

If I cease not to pray

There is no way I can go astray.

If (continued)

If I trust him

He will shield me and not condemn.

If day and night, God I chase

Then on me, he will have mercy and grace.